Train Ride

by Miriam Sklar

ISBN: 978-1-338-75084-3
Illustrated by John Lund

Published by Scholastic Inc., 557 Broadway, New York, NY 10012

10 9 8 7 6 5 4 68 25 26 27/0

Printed in Jiaxing, China. First printing, January 2021.

I see a house from the train.

I see a tree from the train.

I see a river from the train.

I see a boat from the train.

I see a bridge from the train.

I see a building from the train.

I see Grandma from the train!